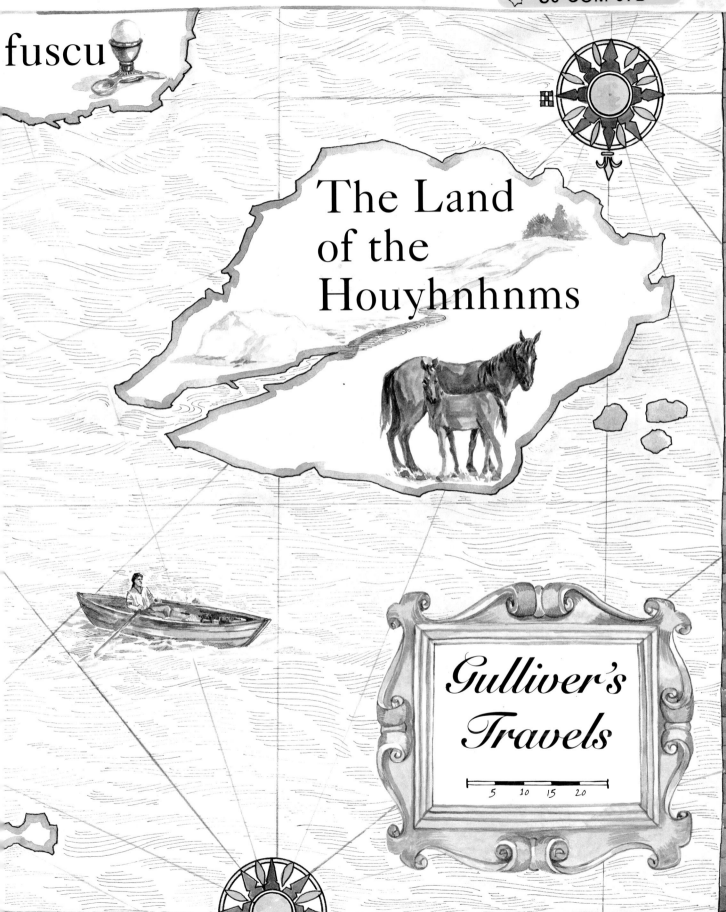

fuscu

The Land
of the
Houyhnhnms

Gulliver's
Travels

5   10 15 20

S0-COM-972

ISBN 0 86112 985 7
© Brimax Books Ltd 1995. All rights reserved.
Published by Brimax Books Ltd, Newmarket, England CB8 7AU 1995.
Printed in Hong Kong.

Jonathan Swift

Gulliver's Travels

Adapted by John Escott
Illustrated by Kim Palmer

Brimax · Newmarket · England

Gulliver's Travels,

first published in 1726, was written by Jonathan Swift.

The satirical story tells of Lemuel Gulliver's extraordinary adventures in the imaginary lands of Lilliput, Brobdingnag and the Land of the Houyhnhnms. Jonathan Swift used satire to make people think about the foolishness of many of the things they did or believed.

Following a shipwreck, Gulliver is washed ashore in Lilliput, where the people are six inches high and the landscape is in proportion. Here Gulliver is a giant.

Gulliver next finds himself in Brobdingnag, where everyone is as tall as a church steeple and he feels like a Lilliputian.

Finally Gulliver visits the Land of the Houyhnhnms where the most important inhabitants were not people, but horses. The horses thought in a totally logical manner and they kept Yahoos as farm animals. The Yahoos were really people who couldn't think or behave in a civilised way.

CONTENTS

PART ONE

A Voyage to Lilliput   9

PART TWO

A Voyage to Brobdingnag   27

PART THREE

A Voyage to the
Land of the Houyhnhnms   45

PART ONE
A VOYAGE TO LILLIPUT

MY FATHER had a small estate in Nottinghamshire and I was the third of five sons. I went to Cambridge to study medicine but my father could not afford to keep me there, so instead I became an apprentice to a surgeon. ❧*But it was always in my mind to travel …*

On May 4th, 1699, I joined the ship *Antelope* at Bristol, as ship's doctor, sailing under Captain Pritchard for the South Seas.

I will not write down everything that happened those first weeks of the voyage, but on our way to the East Indies, we were driven by a violent storm to the north-west of Van Diemen's Land. Twelve of our crew were already dead – from bad food and overwork – and the rest were very weak.

On the 5th November, which was the beginning of summer in those parts, and with the weather very hazy, one of the seamen saw a rock within yards of the ship. There was nothing we could do. The wind was so strong we were driven on to the rock and the ship immediately sank. Six of us managed to get a small boat into the water and began to row, but we were too weak and within half an hour the boat was overturned.

What became of the others, I do not know. I believe they were all lost. As for me, I swam for as long as I could and, just as my strength was giving out, I found I could stand and walk in the water.

It was nearly a mile before I got to the shore of an island, then I struggled a further half a mile before dropping, exhausted, to the ground.

I slept sounder than I had ever done before, then woke at daylight, about nine hours later. I found I was lying on my back but, when I tried to get up, I could not move! My arms and feet were fastened to the ground on each side, and my hair tied down in the same way. More strings had been passed across my body from my armpits to my thighs. The only thing I could do was lie there.

The sun grew hotter and hotter and the light hurt my eyes. There were confused noises around me but, not able to move, I could see nothing but the sky. Then something alive climbed on to my leg! It came over my body and up as far as my chin where I was just able to make out what it was – *a tiny man less than six inches high*! He had a bow and arrow in his hands and a quiver at his back. Suddenly, forty more of these tiny creatures followed him!

I was so astonished that I roared loudly, and they all ran back in fright. Some were hurt in the scramble to jump off me, I learned later. However, a few soon returned, and one came as far as my face.

"*Hekinah degul!*" he cried out in a clear voice, and the others repeated the same words. But what did they mean?

I managed to break some of the strings that tied my left arm to the ground, then pulled some of my hair loose so that it was possible to turn my head. This frightened the little men and they ran some distance away before turning to shoot arrows at me. Hundreds of them fell like tiny needles on my face and hands, and I was afraid for my eyes.

I knew now that I could easily free myself if I wanted to, but it seemed wisest to lie quietly until night-time. For an hour after that, I heard the sound of men working nearby and, later on, about fifty of them cut the strings which

held the other side of my head. Now I was able to turn and see what was happening.

They had built a platform one and a half feet high, with ladders to reach it. It was big enough for four people to stand on and one of these began a long speech in their strange language. I listened, and although his words were strange I could sense that they were not all unfriendly, so I pointed to my mouth to show him that I was very hungry and needed food. The last food I had eaten had been aboard ship, and that had been many hours ago.

He understood me and commanded that ladders should be put against my sides. This was quickly done, then more than a hundred of the little men brought baskets of meat and bread. The loaves were so tiny I ate them three at a time! They brought me a barrel of their wine which I drank in one gulp, but after the second barrel there was no more.

The little people were so amazed by all this that they began to dance and sing on my body crying, "*Hekinah degul*!"

After some time, a person of high rank who had come from their Emperor climbed on to my body and began to speak to me, pointing in the direction of what I was later to discover was their capital city. He seemed to be telling me the Emperor wanted to see me. I tried to tell him I wanted to be set free but he would have none of this and made signs that I would have to be carried as a prisoner.

After he had gone, a number of the people loosened some of the cords on my left side so that I could turn more freely. Then they put ointment on my face and hands to take away the soreness their arrows had caused. Soon after, feeling more relaxed after my food and drink, I fell asleep. (I learned later that the Emperor had ordered them to put a sleeping potion in the wine.)

During the time I slept, five hundred carpenters and engineers were set to work on a large platform with wheels. The platform was over seven feet long and stood three inches off the ground. It took nine hundred of the little men to lift me on to it, using a series of ropes and pulleys.

Fifteen hundred of the Emperor's largest horses pulled the platform on the long march to the capital city, resting overnight and moving on again at daylight. At noon, we arrived about two hundred yards from the city gates. Thousands of people had come to the gates to see me.

There was a church close to the place where we had stopped – the largest building in the whole kingdom – and it had been made ready for me to use as a place to sleep in. The doors would be just big enough for me to crawl through.

Next, eighty of their tiny chains were attached to my left leg, so that I could not move far away, and then the little men cut the rest of the strings.

At last, I was able to stand up.

Gasps of astonishment swept over the huge crowds of people who had come from the town. They stared at my great height, pointing and talking to one another in amazement.

I looked about me. The countryside around was like one enormous garden, the fields about forty feet square, with trees no more than seven feet high.

The Emperor, who had been watching from a high tower, came on horseback to see me. His horse became startled at the sight of me and reared up, but the Emperor managed to stay in the saddle until helped down by some of his servants. He was a tall man with a sword in his hand, dressed in fine clothes and wearing a light helmet of gold and diamonds.

He walked around me, keeping a safe distance, then ordered food to be brought. It arrived in carts which were pushed forward until I could reach them, each containing two or three good mouthfuls.

The Empress and the young Princes also came to watch me eat. Several times the Emperor spoke to me and I replied, but neither of us could understand the other. After about two hours, he and the court went away, leaving me guarded by soldiers.

Some of the crowd shot arrows at me as I sat on the ground, one arrow narrowly missing my left eye. The guards took six of these men and tied them up, then they handed them over to me to punish as I wished. I put five of them into my pocket, then pretended to be about to eat the sixth.

The poor man screamed with fear, and the guards looked frightened when I took a penknife from my pocket. But I cut the strings around the man and put him gently on the ground, where he ran away. I did the same with the other five, and this act of mercy seemed to please both the soldiers and the people in the crowd.

News of my arrival spread quickly throughout the kingdom and people came long distances to see me. Meanwhile, the Emperor held meetings with his advisers to try to decide what to do with me. Some feared I would break loose and be dangerous; others were worried about the great cost of feeding me and whether doing so would start a famine.

Then news of my kindness to the six men was brought to the Emperor and it was agreed to keep me alive. People living close to the city were ordered to bring me six cows and forty sheep each day, together with bread and wine. Three hundred tailors were told to make me a suit of clothes; and six of the cleverest men in the kingdom were instructed to teach me their language.

Within three weeks, I was able to understand and speak with the Emperor, and the first thing I asked was to be set free. But they were not ready to release me yet.

"In time, perhaps," said the Emperor. "But first I would like to have you searched. You may be carrying dangerous weapons."

I assured him I wasn't but told him he could have me searched if he liked. So

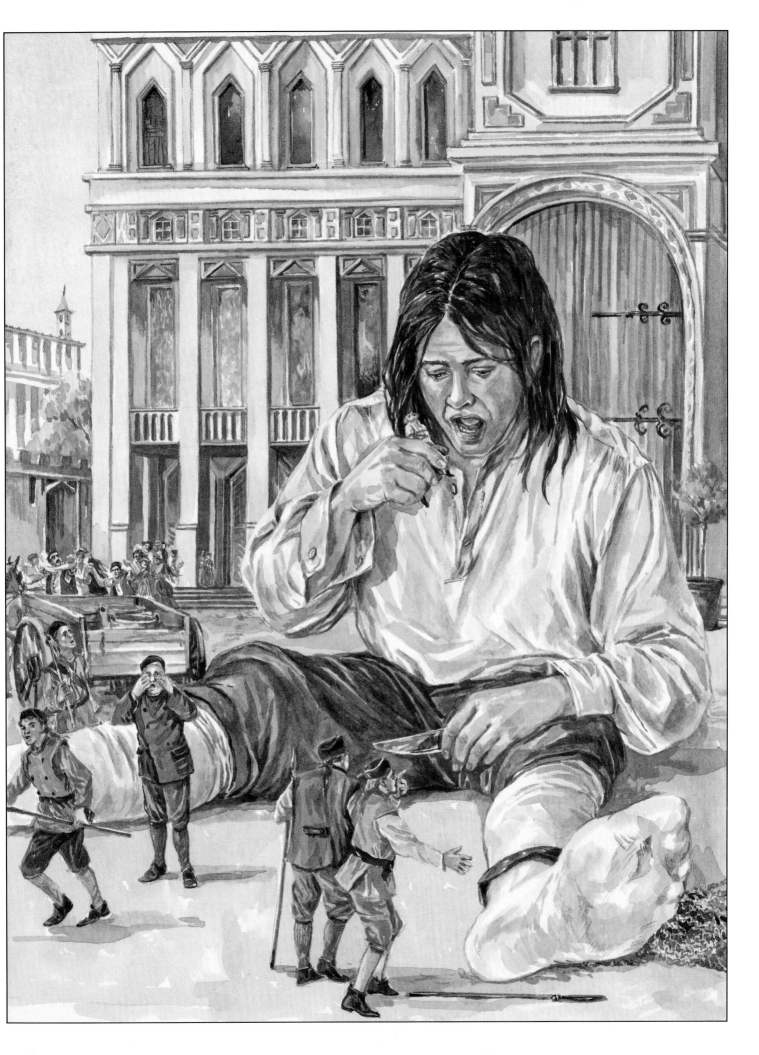

two of his soldiers were called and I lifted them up in my hands and put them first into the pockets of my coat. After this, I put them in all my other pockets – except for one secret pocket which I did not want searched.

They made a list of their findings:

A handkerchief – "a large piece of cloth, big enough to be a carpet in your Majesty's state room."

A snuff box – "a huge silver chest filled with a powder which made us sneeze."

A notebook – "a bundle of white, thin material tied with strong cable and marked with black figures."

A comb – "a machine for combing the great Man-Mountain's head but which looks like the fence around your Majesty's court."

My knife, pistols, razor and watch were too strange for them to identify in any way. And they thought the coins in my pocket must be hugely valuable if they were real gold.

My sword was as long as five of their men, and it was the first thing the Emperor made me surrender. Then he asked what my pistols were for.

"I'll show you," I said, "but don't be afraid."

And I took one and fired it into the air. Hundreds of people fell down as if they had been struck dead, and even the Emperor looked frightened. I gave up both pistols but warned him that the powder and bullets should be kept away from the fire, otherwise it would blow his imperial palace into the sky.

He took these weapons from me but returned the rest of my things. Also, in the pocket which they had not found or searched, I had a pair of spectacles. These I kept a secret.

Slowly, the little people became less afraid of me and I began to have real hope that I might soon be allowed to go free. Entertainers were sent to amuse me, riders jumped their horses over my hands and feet or performed military displays for me to watch.

Two or three days before I was set free, some of the people had found a strange black object lying near the place where I had first come ashore. They hurried back to tell the Emperor, who listened nervously.

"It's as wide as your Majesty's bedroom!" said one of the men.

"And as high as a man," said another.

"And it's hollow inside," said a third.

"It's my hat!" I said, smiling. "I thought I had lost it at sea. Please can you bring it to me?"

They did bring it, but it was no simple job. They had to make two holes in the brim, then use rope to harness it to some horses so that it could be dragged along the ground.

At last, the Emperor agreed to allow me my freedom provided I would obey certain instructions. They were:

1. *That I should not leave Lilliput without their permission.*
2. *That I should only go into the city after they had given me permission and after the*

people living there had been allowed two hours to shut themselves inside their houses.

3. That I should only walk on roads and not through fields, nor should I lie down on them.

4. That I should take care when walking not to tread on any animal or person, nor to pick them up.

5. That I should help them in the war against the people of the Island of Blefuscu, and to help destroy their ships.

6. That I should help workmen with the lifting of large stones as they built a wall around the royal park and palace.

7. That I should measure the size of the island by walking around it and counting my steps.

8. Lastly, that if I agreed to these terms, I would be given enough food and drink each day to satisfy 1724 of their people.

I agreed to all these things and my chains were removed.

A VOYAGE **III** TO LILLIPUT

❧The first place I wanted to see was the capital city. The Emperor agreed and a warning was given out that I was coming. People were told to stay inside their houses for safety.

I stepped over the Western Gate and passed gently through the two main streets. The tops of the buildings were crowded with people who had come to watch me. Heads poked through open windows, noses pressed against glass. I could not enter the lanes and alleys, only look along them, but I could see that the shops and markets were thriving.

The Emperor's palace was in the centre of the city where the two main streets met, and I had the Emperor's permission to step over the outer wall and into the courtyard, where I saw the tall palace building. By lying down on my side, I could look through the lower windows where the Empress and the young Princes smiled at me.

It was two weeks later when an important friend of the Emperor came to see me.

"For many years," he told me, "there has been a quarrel going on between many of the Lilliputians. You will have noticed that some of the people wear high heels on their shoes, and others wear low heels. The high heeled people are called Tramecksans, and those with low heels are Slamecksans. It has been the Emperor's custom only to allow low-heeled people to work for him. And, indeed, his Majesty's heels are lower than anybody's. But this situation causes a great deal of argument. Tramecksans will not sit or eat with Slamecksans, nor will the two sides talk to one another."

Then he told me of a much greater threat to the peace of his country.

18

"We are at war with the people of Blefuscu," he said.

"What's this war about?" I asked.

"It's about the very important matter of how we break an egg before eating it," he said solemnly. "A long time ago, when the Emperor's grandfather was a boy, he was about to eat an egg by breaking it at the biggest end when he cut one of his fingers. Immediately, the Emperor of the time made a law commanding all his people to break only the smaller ends of their eggs in future or they would have to leave Lilliput. Many thousands refused to obey the law and they went to live on the island of Blefuscu. Since that time, there has been continuous quarrelling between the two countries. Now they're about to attack us with many ships and his Majesty wants you to help us."

"Tell the Emperor that, as a foreigner, I cannot interfere in the affairs between two empires," I said, "but I'll be happy to defend him and his people against the invaders."

It was possible to see the island of Blefuscu from the north-east coast of Lilliput and, lying down behind a hill, I looked thoughtfully across at the fleet of warships anchored in their harbour. Then I went back to my house.

Soon after, I asked for a large quantity of the strongest cable and bars of iron to be brought to me. When it came, I made hooks with the iron which I then tied to the cables. Then I went back to the north-east coast and, taking off my shoes and stockings, walked into the sea.

It was low tide and took just half an hour to reach the enemy ships. When the seamen saw me coming, many of them leapt into the water and swam ashore to join the thousands of others who were watching me with terror.

I fastened hooks to the prows of each warship and tied all the ends of the cords together. As I did this, the enemy shot thousands of arrows into my face and hands, the pain was terrible. Once again, I was afraid for my eyes but then I remembered my spectacles in the secret pocket, and quickly took them out and put them on.

Next I cut the anchor cables which held the ships, then gathered up the knotted ends of my own cables and walked out to sea, pulling fifty of their largest warships behind me. The islanders could only watch helplessly.

When I was a safe distance from Blefuscu, I pulled the needle-sharp arrows from my face and hands and took off my spectacles again. Then I walked on to Lilliput.

The Emperor and his whole court were waiting for me on the shore. So delighted was the Emperor that he immediately made me a nardac, the highest rank of honour in their country. But his delight did not last long.

"Please, return and capture the rest of the enemy fleet," the Emperor begged me, "so that I can make slaves of the people of Blefuscu and put an end to the war once and for all."

"I can't do that," I told him. "I can't use my great strength to make slaves of free men and women. It would be wrong."

He was not pleased, and afterwards some of the Emperor's closest advisers – including the admiral of the Lilliput fleet who was jealous of my success against

20

Blefuscu – used my refusal to go back to Blefuscu as an excuse to turn the Emperor against me. Many of these men had hated me since my arrival in their country, and now they had a way of persuading the Emperor I could not be trusted and that I might be dangerous to them in the future.

Three weeks later, important men from Blefuscu came to Lilliput with an offer of peace. I did what I could to persuade the Emperor to agree to it and not be too harsh on his former enemies. Even so, he would only agree after he had taken land, ships and other property from the defeated empire.

Nevertheless, these important men of Blefuscu were grateful for my help in getting a peaceful settlement and invited me to their island so that their people could see how big and strong I was.

"I will be pleased to come," I said, "but first I must get the permission of the Emperor of Lilliput."

It was not easy. Although the Emperor gave his permission, I could see he was angry about it. And later that night, one of the Emperor's wise men who was my friend came to my house with a warning for me.

"Some of the Emperor's advisers have persuaded his Majesty that you are an enemy of Lilliput," he told me, "and that the visit you plan to make to Blefuscu will be used to make war on us. In other words, they're calling you a traitor!"

"But it's a lie!" I cried.

"Nevertheless, the admiral of the fleet, the treasurer and several others wanted you to be put to death by setting fire to your house when you were asleep," he said. "The Emperor would not agree to this, but he's given orders for his men to put out your eyes and make you blind as a punishment! And there are secret plans to slowly starve you to death by stopping your food."

I could hardly believe it and at first was very angry. I wanted to use my superior strength to destroy the capital of Lilliput and all who lived there. But then I began to think of all the kindnesses the Emperor and most of the people had shown me when I had first come to the island, and I knew I could not do it. There was only one thing to do, I decided. Leave Lilliput for Blefuscu immediately.

I went to the north-east shore of the island. Here I seized a large warship, tied a cable to its prow and lifted its anchor. Then I took off my clothes and put them in the ship, together with all my other possessions, to keep them dry. After this, I walked and swam through the sea to Blefuscu, pulling the warship after me.

The Emperor of Blefuscu was pleased to see me. He and his people made me welcome on their island, although there was no building large enough for me to make into a home and I was forced to sleep in the open.

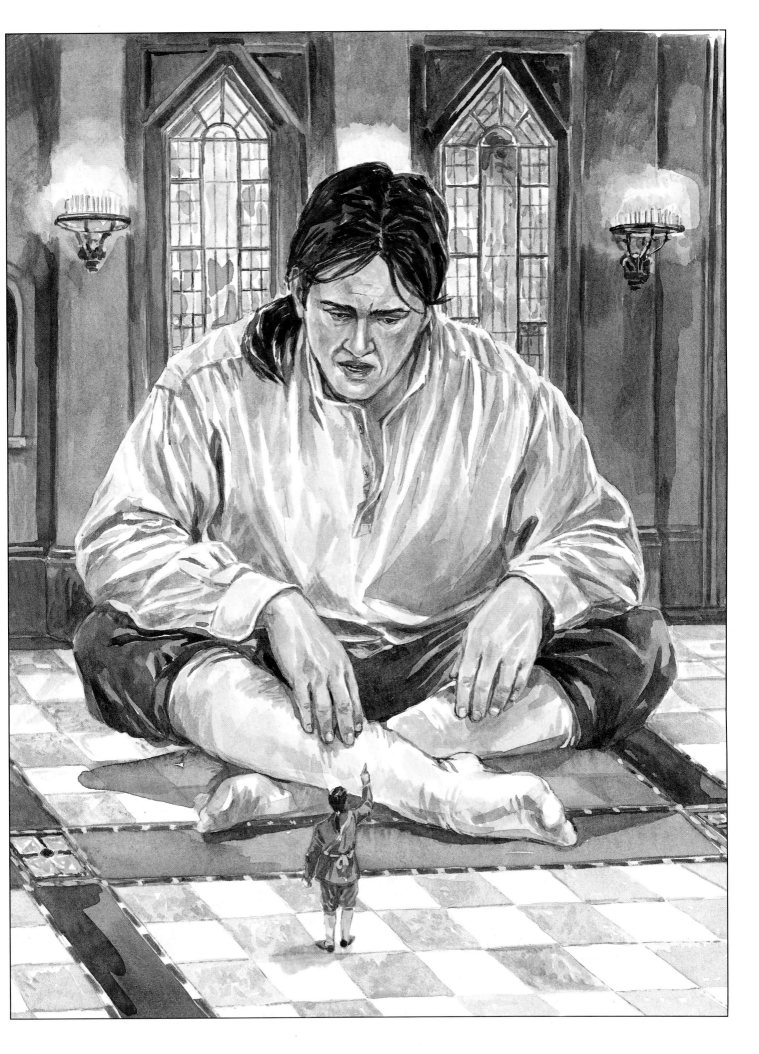

Three days after my arrival on the island, I was walking along the north-east coast when I saw what looked like a boat, floating out at sea. I quickly pulled off my shoes and stockings and waded out into the water. As I got closer to the floating object, I became even more certain that it was a real, full-sized boat. Probably one that had been washed off a ship in a storm and then lost.

I hurried back to the beach and went quickly to the Emperor. I told him what I had seen, then said, "Please lend me twenty of your largest ships and three thousand of your men to help me bring this boat ashore."

He was happy to agree to this and soon after the fleet set sail. Meanwhile, I went back to the coast via the shortest route. To my delight, I saw that the tide had driven the boat even closer to the shore.

As soon as the Emperor's ships arrived, I waded and swam out to the boat. The seamen threw cables to me and I tied them to the boat, after which the ships pulled and I pushed it towards the shore.

We left it in shallow water and waited for the tide to go out again. When this happened, the boat was left on dry land and with the help of two thousand men I turned it up the right way.

It was quite seaworthy and hardly damaged at all. Over the next ten days, I made some paddles, then rowed it round to the royal port of Blefuscu where a large crowd came to look and wonder at the sight of so large a vessel.

"I want to use the boat to try and get home," I told the Emperor. "Will you help me?"

He agreed to supply me with all I needed to make the boat ready for a journey, for it was my plan to sail to the nearest country where I might find a ship to take me to England. Five hundred workmen were employed to make two sails, whilst I made ropes and cables by twisting together the thickest of theirs. A large stone served as an anchor and tall trees were cut down to make the oars and masts.

In a month, I was ready to leave. The boat was loaded with meat, bread and wine. I also took six live cows and two bulls, together with some sheep, which I planned to show my own people when I arrived home. I also hoped the animals would breed. I would gladly have taken some of the people with me but the Emperor would not allow this and made me promise to take only animals from the island.

On September 24th, 1701, at six in the morning, I set sail.

I was hoping to reach the islands that lay north-east of Van Diemen's Land but something happened before this. Two days after I had left Blefuscu, I spotted a ship to the south-east of me. With great excitement I sailed in her direction and, after half an hour, a flag was flown and a gun fired to show that they had seen me. I was overjoyed.

It was an English ship, on the way home from Japan. The captain was a Mr John Biddel and amongst his crew of fifty men I found an old friend of

mine – Peter Williams. He was able to tell the others that I was an honest and trustworthy man to have aboard. After this, the captain made me very welcome.

He asked me where I had come from and I told him my story. At first he did not believe me, thinking I had been driven crazy after weeks adrift in an open boat. But then I showed him the cows and sheep which I had brought aboard in my pockets and he was forced to believe my tale.

On April 13th, 1702, we arrived in England.

I gave the captain a cow and a sheep as a present, then I made my way home. My wife and family were delighted to see me after such a long time.

I stayed two months and during this time I kept my animals in a park in Greenwich, near my home. Many people came to see them, and before I began my next voyage, I sold them for six hundred pounds.

PART TWO

A VOYAGE TO BROBDINGNAG

TWO MONTHS after my return from Lilliput, I became restless. I wanted to travel again. And so, on the 20th day of June, 1702, I joined the ship *Adventure*, bound for Surat . . .

COGITO ERGO MAXIMUS SUM

For the first few months, it was a good voyage, but then we were at the mercy of one fierce gale after another. During one very bad storm, we were blown so far off course that the captain was forced to admit he no longer knew where we were.

"We have enough food to last us for several weeks," he told us, "but we badly need fresh water."

For days we saw nothing but sea, then almost a year after our departure from England, on the 16th day of June, 1703, a boy on the top mast shouted, "Land ahoy!" And to our great relief we saw he was right, although we did not know what island or country we were approaching.

As soon as we were near enough, the captain sent a dozen of us ashore in one of the ship's boats to find some fresh water. Most of the men searched near the beach, whilst I went inland looking for a river or spring. The land was barren and rocky and I could find no supply of fresh water so, after a while, I made my way back towards the others.

Suddenly, I came to a high point where I could look down on the sea below me, and to my astonishment I saw the men were already in the boat and rowing as fast as possible towards the ship, obviously terrified by something.

I was about to shout to them when I saw the reason for their rapid departure. A huge creature was wading out into the sea! The water came no higher than his knees and he was taking enormous strides in an effort to reach the little boat, plunging his feet into the waves. But the coastline was littered with sharp, pointed rocks which slowed him down, and it soon became clear he was not going to catch my shipmates.

Anxious not to be seen by this giant of a man, I turned and ran into the hills where I could look down on the rest of the countryside around. At first there seemed to be many tall forests, but then I realised the 'trees' were not trees at all but fields of grass or corn – some of the corn almost forty feet high.

I walked and walked until at last I found myself on what seemed to be a wide road but which proved to be no more than a path through a field of corn. I walked on for almost an hour before coming to a hedge one hundred and twenty feet high, and a stile to climb into the next field. I was trying to work out a way of climbing the stile – each step of which was like a high stone wall to me – when I heard a noise. Someone was coming across the other field towards me!

He was as tall as a church steeple, like the man I had seen wading into the sea. Each enormous stride covered ten yards of the field. Then, in a voice like thunder, he gave a shout and seven more of the monsters arrived by his side. They were not so well dressed and were carrying reaping hooks in their hands. Each hook was as big as six scythes.

The first man spoke several more words I could not understand, then the seven others came into the field where I was hiding amongst the corn. To my horror, they began to cut the corn all around me!

I tried to keep out of their way but they came closer and closer, whichever direction I ran. Then one of the reapers moved towards me, his huge foot about to squash me to death.

"Stop!" I screamed.

He heard me and stopped. He looked at the ground around his feet with a puzzled look on his face. Then he saw me lying on the ground and his expression changed to one of surprise. Carefully, as though he was afraid I might bite, he picked me up in his fingers and examined me more closely. I was sixty feet from the ground and became terrified he would drop or throw me down before crushing me with his foot, like some unpleasant insect.

"Please, don't kill me!" I begged him.

He looked pleased to discover I could talk, even if he couldn't understand what I was saying.

"You're hurting me!" I shouted, pointing to my sides where his fingers were squeezing the breath out of me.

He seemed to understand what I meant and, lifting up the hem of his coat, he dropped me into it and carried me across to his master the farmer, the man who had first come into the field.

The two men spoke for a few minutes, then I was placed on the ground in front of the farmer. I spoke to him in several languages but he understood none of them. The other farm hands came to look at me, staring at me until the farmer sent them back to their work. Then he spread his handkerchief on one of his huge hands and signalled to me to climb on to it. It seemed wisest to obey, so I climbed on to the handkerchief and lay down flat so that I couldn't overbalance and fall off. He then wrapped me up in it and carried me home to show his wife.

At the first sight of me, the woman screamed like someone who has seen a mouse, but gradually she began to realise I was quite harmless and became more friendly. It was the middle of the day and they were about to have their dinner. The farmer's children came into the room, then a servant brought in the meal – a large dish of meat, twenty-four feet wide.

The farmer put me on the table, a frightening thirty feet from the floor! I was terrified of falling and kept as far away from the edge as possible. Then the farmer's wife minced some small pieces of meat and some crumbs of bread and put them in front of me on a wooden plate.

"Thank you," I said to her, with a bow. Then I took out my knife and fork and began to eat.

Next, she sent the servant for their smallest cup (which still held two gallons) and filled it with cider. With great difficulty, I picked up the cup with both hands and drank.

At one point during the meal, the farmer's cat came into the room and jumped onto his mistress' lap. It was three times larger than a cow and looked very fierce. I kept well away from it, afraid it might spring at me and snatch me up in its paws. But the cat took little or no notice of me and I was just beginning to relax when a nurse brought in the farmer's baby.

The child immediately saw me and began an ear-splitting wail until the farmer's wife picked me up and held me in front of him. The child grabbed me around the waist and immediately put my head into his mouth. I roared so loudly that he quickly dropped me, and I would have been killed if the mother had not held her apron out to catch me in it.

After the meal was over, the farmer went back to his men in the fields again, leaving me with his wife. I was very tired and, seeing this, she took me to her room and placed me on her bed. She covered me with a clean white handkerchief which was thicker and larger than the sail on a warship, then left me to sleep.

I slept for two hours, dreaming of my wife and children, and when I awoke the memory of this dream made me long for my home and family. But I was alone in the huge room, lying on a bed over twenty-four feet from the floor.

Suddenly, I heard a rustling noise and to my horror I saw two giant rats climbing on to the bed, sniffing at my unfamiliar smell until one came up almost to my face. I jumped up and drew my sword, fighting them off, killing one and sending the other away wounded.

Soon after, the farmer's wife returned and was horrified to see what had happened but relieved to find I was not hurt.

A VOYAGE II TO BROBDINGNAG

The farmer and his wife had a daughter, nine years old. The girl was small for her age, but still more than forty feet high. She was very kind to me, giving me her doll's cradle to sleep in and making me some clothes with the finest cloth she could find (even if it was rougher than sack-cloth against my skin!) She called me Grildrig, a name which her mother and father seemed to like because they called me by it, too. So, later on, did the rest of the people in the kingdom. I called her my Glumdalclitch which I came to understand meant 'little nurse'.

Whenever I pointed at something, the girl would tell me their name for the particular object and I soon began to learn the language this way. We were never apart during the time I was on Brobdingnag, and she saved my life many times.

Slowly, people began to hear that the farmer had found a strange and tiny creature in his field and they became curious. Another farmer, who lived nearby, came to visit my master to see if the rumours about me were true.

"Do you really have a little creature no bigger than a splacknuck?" the farmer wanted to know.

"Yes, indeed!" boasted my master, and he put me on the table. "Walk up and down!" he ordered me, and I did so. "Draw your sword, then put it away again!" he told me, and I did this too.

"Welcome," I said to my master's guest, and I bowed.

The farmer put on his spectacles to see me more clearly. His eyes were like

two full moons shining through windows and I could not help laughing at the sight of them. This made him angry.

"Take him to the market tomorrow," he told my master. "It could be worth your while."

At first I didn't understand what the man meant, but later my little nurse explained to me. At the market I would be treated like a freak, she told me unhappily, and put on show for money. People would pick me up and perhaps hurt me. The thought of this upset her and she tried to persuade her father not to take me, but he would not listen.

Next day, I was taken to the market in the next town. The farmer took his daughter with him, and I was carried in a box which had been made specially. There was a small door in it for me to get in and out, and some air holes so that I did not suffocate. The girl had put a quilt from her doll's bed in the box for me to lie down on, but nevertheless it was a rough and bumpy journey. The farmer's horse took huge steps, and every rise and fall of movement was like being aboard a ship in a great storm.

When we arrived at the market town, my master stopped at an inn where he was well known. He made certain arrangements with the inn-keeper and word was sent out that a strange creature was to be seen at the Green Eagle Inn. I was placed on a table in the largest room and Glumdalclitch stood on a stool beside me to make sure I was safe and to tell me what to do.

Thirty people at a time were allowed in to see me. They crowded round and looked in amazement as I walked about on the table as Glumdalclitch instructed. Then she asked me questions, to which I had to shout the answers so that the onlookers could hear me. Next, I took out my sword and pretended to fight an imaginary dragon, and the crowds were both amused and astonished by all this.

News about me travelled fast and I was forced to repeat this performance twelve times that day, until I was almost exhausted. Once, a schoolboy threw a hazelnut at my head, only narrowly missing me! If it had landed on its target, it would have knocked my brains out for the nut was the size of a large pumpkin. I was pleased to see the boy was punished for his bad behaviour!

The farmer told everyone that he would show me again the next market day, then we travelled back to the farm. Even there I was to be allowed no peace and quiet. As word spread, other farmers, with their wives and children, came from as far as a hundred miles to stand and stare at me.

My master was now making a lot of money from showing me and he decided it would be even more profitable to go to other cities in the kingdom, especially Lorbruglud, their capital city. Preparations were made for the long journey and the farmer instructed his daughter to come with us. Glumdalclitch carried me in a box on her lap as she rode behind her father. The box was tied around her waist and was lined on all sides with the softest cloth she could find so that my journey would not be too uncomfortable.

The farmer stopped at many other cities, towns and villages on the way to Lorbruglud and I was forced to perform in each of them. I soon became tired

and weak. Glumdalclitch, seeing this, pretended to be tired herself so that her father would stop more often and I would have a chance to rest, but it was a long journey and ten whole weeks before we reached the capital city. By this time, I was in very poor health and the farmer began to think I might soon die. But instead of letting me rest, he wanted to make as much money out of me as he could and made me work even harder!

The king and queen had their royal palace in the city and my master had taken lodgings nearby. This was how the queen came to hear about me and a messenger was sent commanding my master to take me to the palace.

The queen was charmed by my good manners and the way I answered her questions.

"Would you like to stay and live at the palace?" she asked.

"I am the slave of my master," I said with a bow, "but I should like to live here very much."

She then asked the farmer to sell me, and paid him a thousand pieces of gold.

"May I ask a favour?" I said to the queen. "I would like my little nurse, Glumdalclitch, to stay here as well."

The queen agreed, and the farmer was happy to have a daughter living at the palace. Glumdalclitch herself was overjoyed.

A VOYAGE III TO BROBDINGNAG

When the farmer had gone, the queen took me to see the king. Although he was a very wise man, he took one look at me and thought I was a toy! But when I spoke, he was astonished.

"Tell me where you come from," he demanded.

"England, Your Majesty," I replied.

"And are all the people in your country small like you?" he asked.

"They are all of a similar size, sir," I said, "and the trees and animals and houses are of a convenient size to match."

After this, he instructed the queen to take special care of me and a carpenter was ordered to make a box for me to use as a bedroom. It was fifteen feet square and twelve feet high, with windows, a door, and two cupboards. The top was hinged so that it could be lifted up and down for Glumdalclitch to clean my 'room' and to take my bed out each day and put it back again at night.

The queen liked my company at dinner and I would sit at a table of my own, just at her left elbow, so that she could watch me. She gave me small pieces of meat which I then cut myself before eating. On Wednesdays, when the royal family all ate together, the king liked me to have my table near him. He and his son, the prince, asked me lots of questions about England, its people and its laws, and I was happy to explain.

The person who angered me most was the queen's dwarf. He was less than thirty feet high but he was rude and pompous, teasing me about my size and playing tricks on me. One day, he dropped me into a bowl of cream on

36

the queen's table! If I had not been a good swimmer, I would have drowned. Luckily for me, the queen was so annoyed with him, she sent the dwarf away from the palace and I never saw him again.

Another time, I was attacked by giant wasps! Glumdalclitch had put my box on a window-ledge one morning, so that I could enjoy the fresh air. I had opened up my own window and was sitting at the table eating my breakfast. The wasps were attracted by the smell of the food and twenty of them came flying into the room, making a noise like bagpipes! I was terrified! These huge insects were the size of eagles and I could see their stings were as sharp as needles.

Several of them swooped down and took away some of my breakfast, others swirled around me until I got out my sword and attacked them in the air. I managed to kill four, but the rest flew away and I quickly shut my window.

I often spoke of my sea voyages to the queen, who was always interested to hear about them. She asked me if I knew how to sail and I told her I did.

"Perhaps you would enjoy rowing or sailing a boat here," she suggested.

"I would indeed," I told her, "but how can it be managed? Your smallest boat is the size of one of our warships and I couldn't handle it alone."

"If you can design a boat to suit you," she said, "I'll have it made."

So this is what I did. And ten days later, a boat was delivered.

The queen had also ordered a wooden trough to be made – three hundred feet long, fifty feet wide and eight feet deep. This was placed in an outer room of the palace and filled with water. Here I could row the boat for my own exercise and pleasure, or the queen would wave her fan or blow across the water to make some wind for the sail.

One mishap occurred when a servant accidentally tipped a frog into the trough when he was refilling it with water. The frog jumped into my boat, almost tipping it over, then hopped backwards and forwards until I was able to push it out of the boat with one of my oars.

But the greatest danger I faced was from a monkey which belonged to one of the kitchen workers at the palace. I was in Glumdalclitch's room one morning whilst she was out. It was a warm day and she had left the window open, and I was in my box sitting quietly beside my table. The window of the box was also open and, suddenly, I heard a sound. I looked out of my window to see a monkey jumping around Glumdalclitch's room.

I tried to shut my own window but the monkey was too quick for me. He reached out with one of his paws and grabbed my coat collar, lifting me right out of my box! I think he thought I was a baby monkey for he treated me quite gently and stroked my face with his paw.

A moment later, there was another sound, this time from the door of Glumdalclitch's room. She was coming back. The sound startled the monkey and he jumped back to the open window, still clutching me in his paw, and scrambled up the side of the building and on to the roof!

I heard Glumdalclitch give a shriek as she saw the monkey carrying me out. After that, a quarter of the palace was in uproar as servants ran for ladders, and

hundreds of people in the Court pointed and shouted as they saw the monkey sitting on the roof, holding me. Some threw stones to drive the monkey down, but this was quickly forbidden in case I was struck by one of them.

Men climbed up the ladders and the monkey, suddenly feeling trapped, dropped me on to a roof tile and made his escape. There I sat, three hundred yards from the ground and expecting every moment to be blown down by the wind, until one of the servants reached out and picked me up. He put me in his pocket and carried me safely to the ground.

The king often instructed his servants to bring my box to him, and it would be placed on a table nearby so that we could sit and talk. He was very curious about my country and I did my best to explain some of our ways and customs. The king listened carefully, frequently taking notes and asking questions. I tried to make my country sound attractive and an admirable place to live, but he did not seem convinced.

In a last effort to please him, I explained about the making of gunpowder, and the advantages to any kingdom lucky enough to have this invention available to them. How, in a case of a war, gunpowder would give his own people superior power over any enemy. I even offered to teach his workmen how to make it.

But far from being pleased, the king was horrified. He had no wish whatsoever to know how to make such a destructive and evil invention at his disposal, he said.

"I would rather lose half my kingdom than know the secret," he told me. "And if you value your life, you'll mention it to no-one else on the island!"

His views of our parliament and government were no less strong.

"Any man who can grow two ears of corn or two blades of grass where only one grew before, will do more good for mankind than a whole race of politicians put together," he announced.

And nothing I said could change his opinion.

A VOYAGE IV TO BROBDINGNAG

After I had been in this country for two years, the king and queen set off on a long journey to the south coast of the kingdom. Glumdalclitch and I went with them, I travelling in my box, as usual. A hammock was fixed by silk ropes to the four corners, so that I should not feel the bumps so much when the servant carried me on horseback.

We stopped at a palace near Flanflasnic, a city near the sea, but the journey had made both Glumdalclitch and I very tired. I had a small cold, but my little nurse was so ill that she had to stay in her bedroom.

I longed to see the ocean, and I knew it would be my only avenue of escape if such an opportunity ever occurred. So I pretended to be worse than I was.

"I need some fresh sea air," I said. "It will make me feel better."

Glumdalclitch instructed a page to take me down to the beach in my box.

"Be very careful with him," she said, tears forming in her eyes as if she already knew what was to happen.

The boy took me down to the seashore and placed my box on a rock. I lay in my hammock and began to doze. The boy, thinking it safe to leave me for a short time, went off to look for birds' eggs amongst the rocks.

Suddenly, I was woken from my half-sleep by a violent tug on the ring handle that was fixed to the top of my box. I felt the box being raised into the air, and then forwards at high speed. The first jolt had shaken me out of my hammock, but now we glided easily along. I looked out of my windows but saw only the sky.

Then I heard a flapping noise overhead and I knew what had happened. A large bird, probably an eagle, had swooped down and picked up my box, taking the ring handle in its beak.

A terrible thought rushed into my mind. This bird would carry me back to its home, drop me on the rocks so that my box would break into pieces, then pick out my body and eat it for food!

But something else took place before this could happen. There was a sudden squawking and flapping of wings. Another bird was attacking the eagle carrying my box. I was tossed to and fro, then all at once I was falling, falling…

It ended with a huge SPLASH! – then darkness as my box dropped below the surface of the sea.

But it rose again and began to float.

My box was strong, but there were several small leaks which I had to stop as best I could. This done, I felt a little safer. But how long would I last without food or water? And what if there was a bad storm?

My box floated for several days and I became increasingly hungry and thirsty. I was sure I was lost and would never be found now. But then came the day when I heard a noise, and immediately after, felt I was being pulled or towed along in the sea. I began to shout for help, in all the languages I knew. There were more sounds, and my box struck against something hard. Moments later, I felt it being lifted from the water.

And then came a shout – in English! "If there is anyone in there, let them speak!"

"I am here!" I shouted back. "I'm an Englishman. Save me!"

"You are safe," the voice replied. "Your box is fastened to the side of our ship. The ship's carpenter will come and make a hole in the box to get you out."

"No need to waste time doing that," I shouted. "One of you put your finger through the ring and lift the box out of the sea. Then take it into your captain's cabin."

There was a great deal of laughter at this, and I heard one or two men say: "Lift the box with a finger! He's mad!"

It was only when the ship's carpenter had cut a hole in my box, and I had climbed out, that I realised I was with men of my own size again! At first, they seemed strange and small after the huge people of Brobdingnag.

The captain, Mr Thomas Wilcocks, took me to his cabin and gave me a drink,

then told me to rest. I slept for some hours, then awoke to be given supper.

I told the captain my story and, when he did not believe me, showed him the ring the queen of Brobdingnag had given me. A ring so large that I wore it around my neck like a collar. I offered to give it to him in return for my passage home, but he would not take it. However, he did accept the huge tooth of one of Glumdalclitch's servants which had been removed by mistake by an unskilful surgeon.

It was on the 3rd day of June, 1706, when we arrived back in England. It all seemed strange – the smallness of the trees and houses, the cattle and the people. I began to think I was in Lilliput again and was afraid of trampling on every traveller I met.

When I came to my own house at last, I lowered my head to go inside, afraid of striking it on the door frame. My wife ran to hug me, but I stooped too low for her to do so.

To begin with, they all thought me slightly mad. Then slowly, after I had told them my story, they came to understand, and my wife begged me never to go to sea again.

But it was not in my nature to stay at home for long…

PART THREE

A VOYAGE TO THE LAND *of the* HOUYHNHNMS

I STAYED at home with my wife and family for about five months. It was a happy time, if only I had realised it, but I accepted an offer to become captain of the ship, *Adventurer*, and that was to take me away yet again . . .

EQUI PER SEMPER

❦We set sail from Portsmouth and all went well for a while. But then several of my men died from a tropical disease and I was forced to get more seamen from Barbados and the Leeward Islands. This was something I was to regret, for I soon discovered that the men I had taken on had once been pirates.

I had fifty men on board and my orders were to trade with the Indians of the South Seas, and to make whatever discoveries I could. But the rogues I had picked up persuaded my other men to join them in taking over the ship. The mutiny began one morning when several of them rushed into my cabin and tied me hand and foot, threatening to throw me overboard if I tried to resist.

There was little I could do, and I was soon their prisoner.

After a while, they unfastened the ropes and chained one of my legs to a place near my bed, then they placed a sentry outside my cabin door. He was told to shoot me if I tried to escape. They gave me food and drink, then took over the running of the ship themselves.

It was their plan to become pirates and to plunder the Spanish ships, but for this they needed more men. They sailed for many weeks, trading with the Indians, but I was kept locked up in my cabin and had no idea where we were going. I expected each day to be my last, for they were always threatening to murder me.

Eight months after the day we had first sailed, they saw land and I was forced to get into the ship's long-boat to be rowed ashore. The men left me on the beach with just my sword as a weapon.

"What place is this?" I asked them.

But they had no more idea than I and were soon rowing back to the ship without me.

Alone and afraid, I walked away from the sea into some trees, and on towards fields of grass and oats. I was careful, half-expecting to be shot with an arrow by an Indian savage. At last, I came to a road where I saw human footprints, but also the tracks of cows and many horses.

Suddenly, I saw several strange animals in a field, and one or two of the same kind sitting in trees. Some saw me and came across, and I was able to study them more closely. Their heads and chests were covered in thick hair, and they had beards like goats. There was a long ridge of hair down their backs and more on the fronts of their legs and feet, but the rest of their bodies were bare. Their skin was a dull brown colour and they had no tails. The females were smaller than the males, with long hair on their heads and little or no hair on their bodies.

Never before had I seen such ugly animals. Just to look at them made me feel ill, so I hurried off along the road hoping I might soon find a cabin or the home of some Indian.

But I had not gone far when I met one of these ugly creatures coming in my direction. Clearly the monster had never seen anything like me before because

he stopped and scowled in a puzzled and confused way. Then he lifted and stretched out his front paw. I was not sure whether he wanted to hurt me or was just curious, but I drew my sword and struck him with the side of the blade. I did not want to use the cutting edge in case I wounded him, for it might well anger the people of this land, I thought, if they found me attacking their animals.

The beast stepped back and roared so loudly that a herd of about forty more came running from the next field. Within moments, I was surrounded by a howling mob making the most threatening faces. I ran to a tree and, with my back to it, kept the mob at bay by waving my sword at them.

Then, quite suddenly and without warning, they all ran away as fast as they could. What had scared them? I wondered, and began to walk along the road again. Looking into the field, I saw a horse.

The animal started a little when he came nearer to me, then stared wonderingly at my face, hands and feet. He walked round me several times, then placed himself directly in front of me so that I could not easily walk on. We stood gazing at each other for several minutes, then I reached out a hand to stroke his neck. But the animal shook his head and put up his left fore-foot to remove my hand. Then he made neighing sounds, three or four times, until I began to think he was speaking to himself in some language of his own.

As he was doing this, another horse – a brown one – came up. The two animals touched each other's fore-foot, then began to make the neighing sounds, as if talking together. They moved a few paces away, walking side by side, backwards and forwards, like two people discussing something. Several times, they looked in my direction, then 'talked' some more.

I decided to continue my journey along the road, to try and find some human being, but as I moved away the first horse, who was a dapple-grey, made a sound that was clearly a request for me to stop. I turned back and walked over to him.

The two horses came close to me. They peered at my face and hands. The grey horse rubbed my hat all round with his fore-foot so that I had to take it off and put it on again. This seemed to astonish both of them. The brown horse touched my coat and looked even more amazed to find it was not attached to me like a skin. He stroked my right hand, and seemed surprised by its colour and softness.

The two creatures seemed so unlike any other horses I had seen, I began to wonder if they were some sort of magicians who, by a magic spell, had turned themselves into horses as a form of disguise.

"Gentlemen," I said, "if you are magicians you will be able to understand my language. Let me tell you that I am an Englishman, left on your shores by pirates who stole my ship. Please let me ride on the back of one of you, as though you were a real horse, and take me to the nearest house or village." I took a knife and bracelet from my pocket. "If you do this, I will give you these."

The two creatures listened in silence until I had finished speaking. Then they neighed to each other, as if taking part in a serious conversation. It was now

clear to me that they spoke a language of their own, and one which if I tried hard I might well learn.

One word was repeated many times – *Yahoo*. I practised it myself, trying to sound as much like a horse as I could, then when they stopped speaking I said it to them:

"Yahoo!"

This surprised them, and the grey horse repeated the same word twice, as if trying to get me to say it with the right accent.

"Yahoo," I said again. "Yahoo."

The brown horse tried me with a second word: *Houyhnhnm*.

This took me longer to learn, but after two or three tries I got it right, speaking it in a horse-like way. The two animals seemed amazed that I should be able to do this.

After some more talk, which seemed to be about me, the two horses touched their fore-feet again and the brown horse left us. Then the grey horse made signs that I should walk in front of him and I decided I had better obey, at least for the moment.

When I walked too slowly to suit him, he said: *Hhuun, Hhuun*. I understood what he meant and tried to show him that I was very weary. In turn, he let me rest.

A VOYAGE TO THE　II　LAND OF THE HOUYHNHNMS

After about three miles, we came to a long building made of timber. The roof was low and covered in straw. I began to feel a little less worried, expecting soon to see some native Indians or other humans.

The horse made a sign for me to go in first, and I did so. Inside was a large room with a smooth clay floor and a feeding trough all the way along one side. There were five horses, three nags and two mares. Some were sitting down but the others were busy cleaning the room or the feeding trough.

The grey horse followed me in and neighed to the others, as if giving orders, then took me through a second room and into a third. In here was a very attractive mare with two young horses, sitting on mats of straw that were neat and clean.

The mare rose from her mat and came to look at me. The word *Yahoo* was repeated several times by both her and the grey horse, then I was led out into a courtyard and across to another building. We went inside and I immediately saw three of those horrible creatures which I had met soon after landing. They were all tied to a beam by strong rope, and were eating some sort of meat, holding it between the claws of their fore-feet and tearing at it with their teeth.

The grey horse ordered one of his servant horses to untie one of the creatures and take it into the courtyard. Then I was made to stand close to it so that the grey horse could compare us. The master and his servant looked at us, then spoke the word Yahoo several times. It was then I understood. The beast beside

me had a human figure. The face was flatter, the lips larger, and there was a coarse hair on the hands and back. Our feet were also similar, although the horses did not know this because I was still wearing shoes.

The horses were especially puzzled by my body which seemed to be quite different to the creature's, but that was because I was wearing clothes.

The servant horse gave me a piece of meat but it smelled so awful that I gave it back to him, as politely as I could. He threw it to the Yahoo, who ate it greedily. Then he tried giving me some oats and a piece of hay, but I shook my head, trying to make him understand I could not eat this sort of food.

'If I don't meet some of my own kind soon,' I thought, 'I'll quickly starve to death here!'

The master horse seemed to sense my disgust with the Yahoo and ordered it to go back to its kennel. Then he put his fore-foot to his mouth, as if asking what sort of food I would find acceptable. I looked around and saw a cow passing by. I pointed to her and made signs that I would enjoy some of her milk. This worked, because I was taken back to the house and given some.

At noon, something like a large sledge arrived, pulled by four Yahoos. The vehicle was carrying an old horse whose left fore-foot was injured. He had come to eat a meal with our horses and was welcomed with much warmth and good manners.

The friends sat together and dined on oats boiled in milk. The grey horse ordered me to stand beside him, then he and his visitor talked about me with great interest. I heard the word Yahoo mentioned many times.

I was wearing gloves at that time, and the grey horse noticed my hands and looked puzzled. He put his hoof on them three or four times, as if to say, 'Can't you make your hands the proper shape?' So I took off my gloves and put them in my coat pocket. This seemed to please them all and I was ordered to speak the few words of their language that I could say. Then, whilst they ate their meal, the master horse taught me the words for oats, milk, fire, water, and some others.

After they had finished eating, the master horse took me to one side and made it clear that he was worried because I'd not had any food. I decided then that I might well be able to make some kind of bread with their oats, and that this, with some milk, might be enough to keep me alive. So I said the word 'oats', in their language, and the master horse ordered one of his servants to bring some.

By grinding the oats between two stones, and adding water, I managed to make them into a sort of cake which I toasted by the fire. Then I ate the cake with some warm milk. In time, I got used to this strange diet, adding fruit and herbs now and then, and sometimes I caught a bird or rabbit in a trap.

When evening came, the master horse ordered a place to be found for me to sleep. It was only six yards from the house, but separated from the Yahoos. I got some straw, covered myself with my own clothes, and slept very well.

I was anxious to learn the language as soon as possible, and my master and his children, and his servants, were all keen to teach me. They thought I was a strange and talented creature for an 'animal', as they considered me.

I began by pointing at things and asking the name, then wrote them down in my notebook. My master was convinced I was a Yahoo, but he couldn't understand how, if this was the case, I could be so clean and well-mannered and able to learn quickly. Because of his curiosity, he spent a lot of time teaching me his language. He was especially puzzled by my clothes, which he thought were part of my body. I was careful not to take them off until I went to bed and to have them on again before anyone saw me the next morning.

My master was eager to discover where I came from, and to find out how I was able to think and learn, unlike the Yahoos whom I resembled. After ten weeks, I was able to understand most of his questions, and within three months I could answer him in his own language.

"I come from across the sea," I told him. "From a place far away where there are others like me. I travelled here in a ship – a great hollow thing made from trees. The others travelling with me were bad men, and they left me on your shores to fend for myself as best I could."

"You are mistaken," he said. "You have said the thing which was not. It is impossible that there could be a country beyond the sea. And there can be no men who can move about on the water in a great hollow thing. No Houyhnhnm alive could make such a vessel."

It was later that I understood what he meant. He did not think I was telling the truth, but there is no word in their language to mean 'lying'. Instead, you said 'the thing which was not'.

After five months, I was able to speak and understand their language quite well. The Houyhnhnms who came to visit my master were hardly able to believe I was a Yahoo, because my 'skin' was different. They meant my clothes, of course.

But my master was soon to learn the secret of these. One morning, one of his servants came to my room before I was awake. He saw my clothes which had fallen to one side, and my shirt which was above my waist. He reported this strange event to his master, and I was immediately ordered to come and give an explanation.

I told my master that in my country we covered our bodies because of the cold weather and because it seemed right to do so. He was mystified by this. Neither he or his family were ashamed of any part of their bodies and did not think it necessary to cover themselves.

At last I was able to make him believe that there was a country far away, over the sea, and that I and fifty other men had travelled the ocean in a 'hollow vessel made of wood'. I told him it was creatures like myself who made this vessel and who governed the country and made the laws. I also said that it was a

surprise to me when I discovered Houyhnhnms who were able to think and speak to one another. And I told him that if I ever got back to my own country, the people there would not believe me – they would think I said *the thing which was not*.

A VOYAGE TO THE   IV   LAND OF THE HOUYHNHNMS

After three years in their country, I came to love and admire the Houyhnhnms and their gentle, friendly ways. But the Yahoos were creatures I could never like. They were cunning, cowardly and cruel besides being dirty and lazy. The Houyhnhnms kept them in huts or sent them into the fields to work. I, on the other hand, was invited into the house when my master had visitors, and was often encouraged to join in the conversation.

Every fourth year, the Houyhnhnms held a Grand Assembly. This lasted for five or six days and there were discussions about the conditions of certain areas, and whether there were shortages of oats or cows or Yahoos. If there were, these were quickly supplied without argument.

One of these Assemblies was held whilst I was there, and my master went to it as the Representative for our area. It was soon after this that he sent for me one morning, earlier than usual, and I saw at once that he was going to find it difficult to tell me something.

After a short silence, he said: "I don't know how you are going to take what I am going to say. At the last Assembly, the Representatives made it clear they thought it wrong that I should keep a Yahoo in my family, especially as I treated him more like a Houyhnhnm than an animal. 'It is against Nature,' they said. 'Such a thing has never been heard of before and it is wrong.' Either I must employ you like the other Yahoos or else you must swim back, I was told. But if I allowed you to mix with the other Yahoos, they said, then there was every possibility that you would become their leader and make war on us, attacking and destroying our cattle."

"No!" I began, but my master stopped me.

"This left the second suggestion," he went on. "But I doubt whether you are able to swim to another country. So, it is my advice that you build one of the wooden vessels which you have described to me in the past. You can have any of my servants, as well as the servants of my neighbours, to help you build it."

I was very upset by this news, and my master was equally sad.

"If it was left to me," he said. "I would be happy to keep you with me for as long as you live."

I thanked him for this, then told my master that it would take some time to build my boat, but that I would only need the help of one of his servants. He very kindly allowed me two months to complete the work.

I began by going back to the beach where the pirates had left me those three long years ago. Then I climbed a small hill and looked in every direction, seeking some sign of land. It was in the north-east that I spotted what looked like

an island, about fifteen miles away. To reach this place, I decided, would be my goal. After that, I would have to trust to luck.

Over the next six weeks, with the help of the servant horse, I made myself a sort of Indian canoe, but much larger. I covered it with the skins of Yahoos, and made a sail from the same material. I made four paddles, then stocked up with food – rabbits and chickens – and milk and water to drink. When everything was ready, I had the boat taken to the beach on a carriage, pulled gently by Yahoos.

My master, his lady and the rest of his family came to see me off. There were many tears, a lot of them my own, for I was very sad to leave. But at last, when the tide was right, I pushed off from the shore.

The wind was kind to me, and I used the sail at first. My plan was to discover some small, uninhabited island and make a home for myself. After living with the kindly Houyhnhnms for more than three years, I no longer wished to return to a land where I would have to mix with Yahoos, as I had come to think of human beings.

By six that evening, I saw what I thought was a small island about two miles away and steered towards it. But it was nothing more than a rock. However, after climbing it, I could see land to the east, stretching from north to south. The next morning, I steered towards this land which was New Holland, and arrived some seven hours later.

I saw no one when I first went ashore, and for three days ate raw shellfish and drank water from a nearby brook to save my own supplies. But on the fourth day, I saw a fire on a hill. And around the fire sat some natives who, on seeing me, chased me back to my boat.

There was no returning to that landing-place, and I paddled away swiftly. But where to go next? I was trying to decide when, quite suddenly, I saw a sail to the north-north-east, coming closer every moment. At first, I wondered whether I should wait for them, but my dislike of Yahoo-humans was so strong that I set off back towards the beach to hide amongst the rocks.

The ship came within one and a half miles of the shore, then sent a small boat for fresh water. I had failed to hide my canoe well enough, and the men who came on the boat quickly saw it. They looked it over and soon decided that the owner could not be far away, then set about finding me.

It did not take them long.

"Who are you?" one asked. He spoke Portuguese, a language I knew well.

"I am a poor Yahoo," I said. "The Houyhnhnms sent me away from their country. Please let me go."

They were pleased to discover I spoke their language but could not understand what I meant by Yahoos and Houyhnhnms. They also laughed at my voice, which by now sounded more like the neighing of a horse than a human voice.

"Where do you come from?" they asked.

"I was born in England," I replied.

"Our captain will take you to Lisbon," they told me. "From there, you can get a ship to England."

The men seemed determined to take me, so there was nothing for it but to go with them. They took me to their captain – Pedro de Mendez – a very kind and polite man. It seemed strange to find a Yahoo so nicely behaved.

I did not want to tell him anything, but he asked so many questions I was forced to tell him my story, beginning with the pirates on my ship and ending with my banishment from the land of the Houyhnhnms. He did not believe me at first, and this made me angry. How could he think I had said the thing which was not? I had spent so much time with the truthful Houyhnhnms, I had forgotten the habit of human beings – to suspect others of telling lies. But at last he believed me and slowly, as the voyage went on, I grew to like him.

We arrived in Lisbon some months later and the captain found me a ship that was bound for England. Two weeks later, that ship sailed, and within another two weeks we arrived in England.

My family were surprised and delighted to see me, for they had thought I was dead. But it took me a long time to learn to live comfortably with humans again, and even today I am angry when I see one treating a horse in a cruel manner.

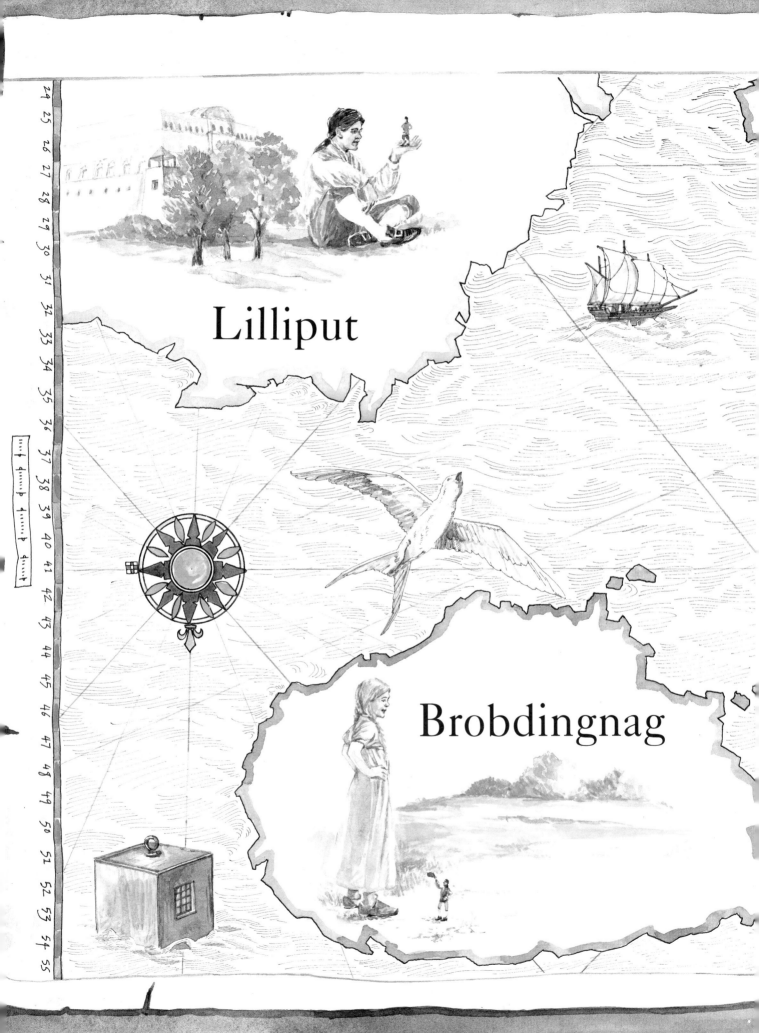

Lilliput

Brobdingnag